# OUR FIRST BLIZZARD SNOWMAN

Lucille Velotta

# Dedication

In memory of my Dad, I wish you were here to see this dream become a reality.

To my Mom, Thank you for being my first friend and greatest champion.

To my siblings, you have given me a fire to continually do better.

To my baby boys, You are my heart and soul. I love you to the moon and back, around the world and back again, to infinity and beyond, always and forever and ever, Amen.

To my Bella, you listen to me and never judge. I love you my baby girl.

To my husband, my love, my life, and my very best friend. Thank you for loving me, supporting me and encouraging me throughout this journey.

Peace, love, joy, good health and happiness to all of you who read this book and share it with your family and friends.

Copyright © 2015 OUR FIRST .

All rights reserved. No part of this book may be used or reproduced by any means, graphic, electronic, or mechanical, including photocopying, recording, taping or by any information storage retrieval system without the written permission of the publisher except in the case of brief quotations embodied in critical articles and reviews.

LifeRich Publishing is a registered trademark of The Reader's Digest Association, Inc.

LifeRich Publishing books may be ordered through booksellers or by contacting:

LifeRich Publishing
1663 Liberty Drive
Bloomington, IN 47403
www.liferichpublishing.com
1 (888) 238-8637

Because of the dynamic nature of the Internet, any web addresses or links contained in this book may have changed since publication and may no longer be valid. The views expressed in this work are solely those of the author and do not necessarily reflect the views of the publisher, and the publisher hereby disclaims any responsibility for them.

Any people depicted in stock imagery provided by Thinkstock are models, and such images are being used for illustrative purposes only. Certain stock imagery © Thinkstock.

ISBN: 978-1-4897-0523-5 (sc)
ISBN: 978-1-4897-0525-9 (hc)
ISBN: 978-1-4897-0524-2 (e)

Print information available on the last page.

LifeRich Publishing rev. date: 09/11/2015

The excitement was building as Vincent and Raymond began to get ready for their first Blizzard. As the snow fell to the ground like feathers floating down from the sky on this cold January morning.

Suddenly, the phone rings and it's a recording from school telling us the news all school age children long to hear,..."school will be closed today due to inclement weather". I turn and look over to the boys, and exclaim "Its A SNOW DAY!!!

The boys were sure to be in for a thrill of a lifetime. A Blizzard Mama? A blizzard? Our very first blizzard! The excitement was mounting all day, it was just too much for their little hearts to take. The pounding of their hearts grew louder, their faces glowing with anticipation, as if someone turned a flood light on in their soul, and it was as bright as the morning sun on a clear summer day. Just glorious and I reveled in each and every minute of watching my babies grow more excited with each passing minute.

Sure not to miss anything, I was armed with my camera in one hand and my video camera in the other hand. I documented every minute of our lives and this was no different. I would work each camera from different angles and I was sure to make this a memory of a lifetime.

Ok let's get ready for our Blizzard Snowman Ray, ok Vin! "Let's do this", they repeated over and over again.

Getting themselves prepared was no easy task, but they were ready for the challenge. Mama we need some help, of course, here are your second pair socks, snow pants, jacket, mittens with warmers and hat. Lastly, your boots, they are always the toughest to get on.

Are we were ready yet? Just about, I said, they looked like two abominable snowmen. All that was showing was the center of their faces still shining bright with excitement.

Ok Ray, let's get our supplies ready; Ok, we have our shovels and buckets.

Are we ready now, Mama? Yes, I believe you are. You may go and build the most perfect Blizzard Snowman you possibly can. As the boys emerged out in to the wintery white wonderland, they were amazed at what they saw, snow covering everything. It was everywhere on the roof tops, on the trees, covering the cars, the streets, even the front porch seemed to disappear under a blanket of white fluffy snow.

It was snowing on us too and as it fell to our cheeks it seemed to slightly dance before landing and melting away. The snowflakes seemed to sit upon my eyelashes before rolling off into my eyes like a small pool of water, a slight stinging happened each time a snowflake landed in my eye. I quickly wiped it away and refocused on the job at hand. Preparing the parts of our Blizzard Snowman was going to be as easy as one, two, three...So we thought!

As we were gathering our snow, rolling it together and trying to create the perfect foundation for our Blizzard Snowman, we soon realized they we were going to need some help and it was time to get the only person who could help us create our perfect Blizzard Snowman. They looked at each other and yelled out "DADDY", of course. Yes it's true, Daddy to the rescue.

"Help us Daddy"! they cried, until he arrived. He was ready and willing to help guide them in their quest of creating the most perfect Blizzard Snowman.

Camera snapping away, video camera rolling and we are ready to gather up the snow. Using our shovels and our buckets to bring the snow closer to where we were about to begin the bottom portion. "Daddy they cried, help us, it's too big"! Daddy "help us", it needs to be bigger and bigger and in minutes it was, Yay, Daddy you're doing it! We jumped for joy all around Daddy and the first part of the snowman was just about completed. All we needed to do was smooth it and round it out. As the snow continued to fall on our cheeks and eyelashes, it ran down our faces, hitting our jackets making a splattering sound, like paint being thrown at a blank canvas. Creating its own unique splattering mark. Our fingers were cold and wet but that won't stop us. Not now, since we are on our way to creating our perfect Blizzard Snowman. "Look Ray, the bottom is so big"! "I know Vin, it's bigger than the both of us".

Daddy suggested that it was time to build the middle of our perfect Blizzard Snowman, so together they gathered up for the belly part of the Blizzard Snowman. They reached far beyond their little arms could stretch, and they stretched some more each yelling to the other S t r e t c h…farther…..and farther then the stretch before the last one. Pulling the snow closer and closer to them. Close enough for them to begin forming the belly. "Do you think we have enough Daddy"? Let's see how it looks on top of the bottom one. One more time they enlisted Daddy's help neither one could lift the belly, it was just too big.

"Your Blizzard Snowman is looking great, boys", Mama called out from somewhere behind them. Being sure not to intrude on their space but close enough to capture the importance of this special event, she continued to take snap shot after snap shot and continued to record each and every glorious minute of us building our perfect Blizzard Snowman. Busy forming the middle like two little worker bees, molding, smoothing, rounding out carefully preparing to place their third and final part of their perfect Blizzard Snowman.

"Ok guys, Daddy said, we need to get the final part ready". Hussle, Hussle… "Let's do this! Let's do this", they exclaimed, as they danced around, clapping their hands, and stomping their feet with pure joy. Yelling out, y e p p i e, y a h o o, over and over.

Gathering up their last bits of snow, the boys notice that the snow was beginning to taper off and their Blizzard Snowman was almost complete. As they continued to gather up some last bits of snow needed for completing the top and final part of their Blizzard Snowman, we asked Daddy for help once again. He reaches over and lifts up this perfectly humungous snowball up in the air, our eyes opened wide in amazement.

Daddy places that big snowball gently on the top of our perfect Blizzard Snowman as if he was lifting up a newborn baby and placing it in its mothers waiting arms. "Here it is boys" Daddy exclaims, "your Blizzard Snowman is all together, but I think Mama has something to make it absolutely perfect." They ran over to me. Mama you have a surprise for us? Yes, as a matter fact I do and I reached behind my back and pulled around to the front of her a bag that contained the finishing touches for our perfect Blizzard Snowman.

They were jumping around with wonder and excitement as to what I had for inside this bag. We peered inside this bag with our eyes as wide as we could open them, we found all the essential parts for putting the finishing touches on our perfect Blizzard Snowman. A hat, but not just any hat, it was a Black Top Hat for his head, a Carrot for his nose, two pieces of coal for his eyes (most likely left over of from our summer BBQ's), a pair of Red Lips for his mouth(I think they were from my Mr. Potato Head), a Corn Cob pipe (could that have been from last night's dinner, I wondered), two branches for his arms (possibly taken from one of the many trees surrounding our house), three very large buttons to put on his belly going straight down the center (I know they were from one of my coats) and a magnificent Black Scarf to wrap around his neck (I am pretty sure it was my scarf too).

Vincent and Raymond yelled, "you've thought of everything Mama"...as I continued to snap away and record this moment of pure joy. Thank you for giving us all of these things to use for our perfect Blizzard Snowman, he looks awesome! Oh yes, he does, I said and Daddy agreed, as well. They stood there like little statues with their faces glowing, redden cheeks and clouds of lite misty smoke that came from their breathe which grew more defined as the night air was beginning to settle in and take over the grey Blizzard day.

The snow was no longer falling and night was creeping in faster, as they stood their admiring their masterpiece. Suddenly the familiar sounds of the outside world were becoming clear. Their senses were beginning to come back to life, the sound of cars passing on the road behind our house, horns blaring at other drivers. Our dog Bella running through the snow we could clearly hear her tiny bell tell us she was close by too.

Each shot I took with my camera seemed so much louder ClickK... ClickK...our laughing even seemed magnified. The snow even had a smell of freshness to it, the snow seemed more wet now in our hands, as it just seeped through our mittens that were completely drenched by the snow; how amazing I thought to myself, just simply amazing.

As they each stood there admiring their perfect Blizzard Snowman, their little faces glowed with excitement and they ran circles around it and calling to anyone who would listen. Each time they heard the crushing of the snow beneath tires that rolled along our street, the mail truck, plow truck, our neighbor who had a monster truck with the biggest wheels I have ever seen. Even a UPS truck was sure to circle around making a few deliveries during our first Blizzard. Our news carrier Zack, pushed through the heavy wet snow just to get a look up close and personal, knowing he must get his deliveries made before night fall he took a few minutes dancing around in joy with us. I am sure it reminded him of a time when he was as happy about completing his first snowman. Each one of them took time to visit us and admire our most perfect Blizzard Snowman.

As Daddy and I stood back and watched the boys' joyous celebration, the snow began to lightly fall once again. Hitting our eyelashes and cheeks and making small pools of water collect on our coats. Our breathe circling out from our mouths, as if we were smoking a pipe. It seemed as though no time had passed at all, nature was telling us something different. Night was beginning to creep in as the sky turned a deeper, darker shade of grey, with shades of pink. The pink that you only see when a snow fall is coming.

It was time to leave our Blizzard Snowman for the night. We wondered what would happen to him...Would he be ok?...Will he be cold?... Will he be lonely?...Should we bring him inside? Don't worry he will be there tomorrow! Daddy and I reassured with each and every question over and over again. Daddy and I felt like we were on a witness stand. YES! NO! YES! NO! It went on for quite a while.

Finally getting inside realizing how cold, wet and tired they really were, but with one more burst of energy they tumbled through the door, busting in to Grandma's room...shouting, Grandma! Grandma! In their loudest voices.......

Did you see him? Did you see him? Did you see our Blizzard Snowman? Isn't he awesomely perfect? Their voices filled with so much excitement and enthusiasm. Grandma couldn't help but be as equally excited and with the loudest voice she could find to match theirs she said, with a childlike giggle in her voice YES, and he is an absolutely, awesomely, perfect Blizzard Snowman. Grandma stood there with the boys for a minute and for just a minute you could hear her giggle like a child and see that childlike sparkle in her eye as she rested in the sound of laughter that filled her room.

They could barely keep their heads up throughout dinner and all the excitement of the day was just too much for them and it was really beginning to catch up to them. We wrapped dinner time up fairly quickly that night. The boys opted out of story time so it was straight to getting in to our cozy PJs, brushing our teeth, prayers and blessings, especially blessing our Blizzard Snowman, followed by Goodnight kisses and hugs. One more look at our Blizzard Snowman before we go up to bed.

P L E A S E...Ok,...Good night to you our perfect Blizzard Snowman. They crept up the stairs slowly, each step seemed to be longer than the one before, becoming more and more sleepy with each little foot step. They quietly reached for their doorknob, too tired to even give it a tug to open, their little feet dragged them over to their beds. It seemed to be in slow motion, as I watched their little arms pull their bodies slowly over the side of their beds, their knees could barely reach up over the edge and with one last tug they were over and as their heads began to lay gently on to their pillows, their eyes began to close and open, open and close, like tiny feathers falling from the sky. Open...close...open...close with each motion their eyelids became heavier with the long nights slumber that was about to enfold them in her arms and off into dreamland. Where they can dream of their most absolutely awesome perfect Blizzard Snowman.